David W. Maull

The Life and Military Services of the Late Brigadier General

Thomas A. Smyth

David W. Maull

The Life and Military Services of the Late Brigadier General Thomas A. Smyth

ISBN/EAN: 9783337183172

Printed in Europe, USA, Canada, Australia, Japan

Cover: Foto ©Raphael Reischuk / pixelio.de

More available books at **www.hansebooks.com**

THE LIFE

AND MILITARY SERVICES

OF THE LATE

Brigadier General Thomas A. Smyth.

By D. W. MAULL, M. D.

Formerly Surgeon in Chief, 2d Division, 2d Army Corps.

INTRODUCTION.

———

THESE Memoirs originated in the action of the Delaware State Historical Society, which in the year 1866, actuated by a laudable State pride in the reputation of its patriot dead, and by a desire to preserve in its archives the records of such fallen heroes, by resolution, invited the author to prepare an essay upon "The Life and Military Services of Brigadier General THOMAS A. SMYTH," to be read at a future meeting of the Society.

In addition to this stimulus to engage in the labor, there was another one in the fact that the friends of Gen. Smyth generally desired, in a more connected and compact form than editorial comments, letters of newspaper correspondents, general orders, congratulatory addresses, press dispatches and written military reports could shape, some narrative of his life; a kind of aggregation of many of the favorable notices and acknowledgements of military services rendered, he had received from both commanders and troops.

The task was a labor of love, and was accepted, if not with confidence, at least with the will and intent to chronicle as faithfully as possible with the means at command, the career of the gallant soldier, and to represent him as he appeared in the estimation of those who knew him best in that field in which he so signally distinguished himself.

The task completed, the results were given in these reminiscences, at a meeting of the Historical Society convened for the purpose.

Though at the time, many of the General's friends—ever anxious to keep the impression of his deeds fresh upon the minds of the community—desired and advised the publication of these Memoirs, no active steps were taken in this direction. But latterly some parties, feeling assured that it was due to the General's memory that the narrative of his life should be given to the public, and satisfied that such a narrative would find a ready sale, not only among his old comrades in arms, who have never ceased to feel a deep interest in all that has pertained to him, but among his friends generally, who admired his course and rejoiced in his renown, solicited these papers with the view to their publication.

With no interest in the enterprise save to acquit ourself as the friend and biographer of a brave man, we shall feel that it was a pleasure to have striven to do justice to his revered memory by collating the main facts and circumstances which made him a hero.

OCTOBER, 1869.

MEMOIR.

IF to secure the gratitude of a people by a military career of high reputation in its service, to develop the qualities of a hero in its behalf, to reflect an honor upon his State by a line of life marked by a succession only of brave deeds, to show a pure and unselfish patriotism, and then yield his life a willing sacrifice to his adopted country, entitle one to be commemorated, the late Brigadier General Thomas A. Smyth is eminently worthy of such a distinction.

His active agency in the addition of some pages to History has acquired for him the right to become historic, and to secure for himself honorable mention in the annals of Delaware; and having shed some lustre on the records of the late war, it is just that he should be reflected in those chronicles. His claims upon posterity for the honor and perpetuation of his memory will be enforced by a recognition of qualities in him which inspired respect, made him deservedly popular with his fellow-men, and caused his death to be regarded as a national loss, by the almost romantic incident and interest with which he had invested a noble life, and by the present high estimate of a fame which is cherished not only by the thousands that served with and under him, and

is as dear to them as their honor as soldiers, but by those
at home who watched his upward course with so much
pride and pleasure.

In gallantry and extent of service towering above all
who represented this State in the army, he will be remembered as a prominent, central figure, upon whom
much attention was concentered, and who became the
theme of praise for many tongues; as one who made
himself illustrious, having distinguished himself by his
valor, and who, without adventitious aids, as high social
status or influence of party, but by mere force of the commanding qualities inherent in him, grade by grade, elevated himself to the position which he so richly merited
and which he so ably filled.

The main points of his history prior to the commence-
ment of his military course, are the only ones that need
be adverted to in this connexion, and that very briefly.
It is his soldier-life that is to be more fully noted.

The subject of this memoir was born on December
25th, 1832 in Ballyhooly, County of Cork, Ireland. His
parents were Thomas and Margaret Smyth: his Father
was a farmer, in which business the son assisted after
leaving school. His advantages for acquiring an education were limited, but by means of travel through Eng-
land and Scotland, and a considerable stay in London
and Paris, he managed to glean a certain knowledge of
the world which he made available in later life.

Having come to this country in August 1854, he set-
tled in Philadelphia, where he followed the business of
carving, and where he remained until the promise of the
excitement, and a leaning to military life, influenced him

to join Walker's forces in Nicaraugua. It is fair to pre-
sume that his experiences in that irregular contest were
not of the most agreeable character, as he carefully
avoided referring to them : certain it is, he was glad to
return to the States.

In the early part of the year 1858, he made Wilmington his home, and on July 7th of the same year, was
married to Miss Amanda M. Pounder. In this city he
was living when the war broke out. Having previously
been an officer in a Militia Company here—the First
National Guards, he considered that it was peculiarly
fitting that he should identify himself with some military organization for active service in the field.

Accordingly in April, 1861, feeling it a duty he owed
to the country of his adoption to aid it in its trials, he
raised in this City a company for the three months service, expecting to have it accepted by Delaware ; but
finding that there would be delay, and becoming impa-
tient at the inactivity or indifference of the State author-
ities, he took his company to Philadelphia, where it was
accepted as Co. II. in the 24th Pa., Vols., Col., afterwards
Brig. Gen. Joshua T. Owen commanding.

During his connection with this organization, very
little opportunity was afforded him to display those military qualities which subsequently made him so conspicuous. The Regiment, much of the time, was encamped
in Maryland or Virginia, near the Potomac, and did little
real service, save watching fords and getting ready for
more active work. But even in this line of duty he
showed himself worthy of confidence, and caused those
who observed his course to feel that he was in earnest :

and Gen. Owen remarked long after, to the writer of
these pages, that he found Smyth to be a man of remarkable judgment, tact and penetration, and that his bravery
and prudence always influenced him to send Captain
Smyth out on any expedition where danger was likely
to be encountered: and he additionally remarked that
his trust in this officer was so implicit, that he had no
doubt he had sometimes imposed on the young man
labors that others should have shared: but that this
officer never complained of the many duties of the kind
he was called upon to perform, but discharged them
faithfully, understandingly and cheerfully. Subsequently these two Generals served in the same Division, and
were much together.

After the muster out of the Regiment, Capt. Smyth
returned to Wilmington where he found the First Delaware Vols. reorganizing for three years service. Without having made any effort to urge his claims upon that
command, he was, Oct. 2d., chosen Major and entered
promptly upon his duties with the Regiment then encamped at Hare's Corner, and soon, by his urbanity,
made himself popular with officers and men.

During the stay of the Regiment at Fortress Monroe,
embracing the time from the latter part of October to
May, the Major remained at his post, devoting himself
with ardor to the drilling of the men. Here was a good
opportunity for him to study military science, and he
took advantage of it. There was nothing here however
to call out his latent genius.

Passing over the capture of Norfolk and the occupa-
tion of Suffolk, we find little incident until the Battle of

Antietam. Before that event, Major Smyth was only known as an excellent officer on drill, vigilant on picket, prudent in little expeditionary movements, very conscientious in the discharge of his duties, and withal a clever gentleman.

But the fight at Antietam demonstrated that he possessed other attributes of a military man, as he, on that occasion, displayed great personal bravery, and promptly opened the eyes of the Reg't to the fact that a man of courage was among their number; and though he was in too subordinate a position to attract much attention as a man of mark, from those above him, he had not failed to cause the members of the command to canvass his merits, and he then laid the foundation for that confidence which the First Delaware ever afterwards reposed in him: the men had correctly gauged him, and found he was ready to lead them wherever he desired them to go.

At the Battle of Fredericksburg, he added materially to this reputation. The 1st Delaware under his command was detailed to act as skirmishers, and as such opened the engagement in front of that Division.

The reports of his superior officers on that occasion may be accepted as the best testimony of his conduct. Col. Andrews, in his official report, says " having already testified to the good conduct of those under my immediate command, it becomes my duty also to state that the First Delaware Regiment detached as skirmishers, were reported as having behaved with great courage and endurance : that after driving the enemy's skirmishers, they sustained alone their fire for a considerable time before the supporting column arrived, and after spending all their ammunition, they retired in good order. Major T. A. Smyth in command is represented as having displayed much coolness and ability." Lieut. Col. Marshall of the 10th N. Y. Vols. who commanded the Brigade subsequently, says in his report, "The 1st Reg't Del. Vols. deserves particular mention for the manner in which, as skirmishers, it opened the engagement and remained on the field until every cartridge was expended," and among other officers mentioned as having behaved with distinguished bravery, Major Smyth's name appears.

The following is an excerpt from Major Smyth's report; " was ordered to report to Brig. Gen. Kimball commanding First Brigade, who, in turn, ordered the Reg't to the front as skirmishers, and informing me that Col. Mason who was General officer of the day, commanding the picket, would direct me to my position. At 12 M. the Reg't marched out the Rail Road, crossing the canal bridge under a severe fire: deploying the Reg't to the left and forwarding, we forced back the enemy's pickets into their rifle-pits; still under a heavy fire of grape, cannister, musketry and shell; took a position under the brow of the hill, this side of the stone wall, where we lay for one hour without being reinforced, and which position our men held until 4 P. M., during which time they expended all their ammunition, receiving fresh supplies from the troops coming up."

On the 18th of December, at a meeting of the officers of the Regiment, he was unanimously elected Lieut. Col. to fill the vacancy occasioned by the resignation of Lieut. Col. Oliver Hopkinson, and on the 30th of the same

month he was commissioned by the Governor. Another
promotion soon followed, for Col. John W. Andrews
having resigned, Smyth was commissioned as Colonel
on the 7th of February.

Col. Smyth was favored at Chancellorsville with a fine
opportunity to develop more fully the gallantry that had
been cropping out in the previous fights. We cannot do
better than copy his report of that engagement.

" I have the honor to report that in obedience to Gen.
orders No. 37, from Headquarters 3d Division 2d Corps,
the Reg't under my command marched from its camp
near Falmouth at sunrise on the morning of the 28th of
April, having position in the centre of the 3d Brigade.
We moved up the road towards Banks' Ford, near which
place we halted about 11 o'clock A. M. and *bivouacked*
for the remainder of the day and night. At 2 P. M. on
the following day the march was resumed, and crossing
the Rappahannock early in the evening at U. S. Ford,
we moved up the road towards Chancellorsville, halting
within a mile of that place about 11 P. M. On the 1st
of May the Reg't remained in column, under arms, without moving. On the morning of the 2d the enemy began shelling our position, but without effect. Late in the
afternoon, the Reg't was formed in line of battle facing
the right. About six o'clock in the evening, the 11th
army corps having given way on the right, the Reg't was
moved to the left of the Chancellorsville road, four companies being thrown across the road to aid in arresting
the stragglers. After the panic had somewhat subsided,
we received orders from Major Norval to support Captain
Frank's Battery posted in the open field to the right of

the Headquarters of Major General French, one company under command of Captain Smith being thrown forward to the edge of the woods as a picket guard, where
it remained during the night. On the morning of the
3d we were moved by order of Major General French a
short distance to the left, ready to advance to the support
of the 1st Brigade, then moving to reinforce the 3d
Corps heavily engaged with the enemy in front. While
in this position a temporary breast work, formed of knap-
sacks, fence rails and bags of earth was erected as a pro-
tection against the fire of the enemy's infantry. About
7 A. M. the 3d Corps being hard pressed in front, gave
way, and in company with the 132d Pennsylvania Volunteers we advanced to the edge of the woods, where
we encountered the enemy in considerable force and
drove him for the distance of half a mile. Then the
enemy having been reinforced, we halted and held him
in check for about three hours, when the Brigade on our
right gave way, allowing the enemy to gain a position
upon our right flank and rear. Being thus exposed to
a galling fire from three directions, the Regiment changed front to the rear on the 10th Company, in perfect order, and assisted with the fire from one of the Batteries,
repulsed the enemy, when having received orders to retreat, we fell back in good order, and took our position
in the rear of the 1st Brigade. The enemy having range
of our position, opened upon us with shell, upon which
we retired in obedience to orders, into the woods. Having rested for about an hour, we were ordered to the
front to support the 1st Brigade. Taking a position on
the 2d line of battle, we remained there, frequently ex-

posed to a hot fire of shell and musketry, until 3 o'clock on the morning of the 6th, when we took up our line of march to the River. Without halting we crossed the pontoon Bridge at U. S. Ford, and reached our old camp about noon.

" Our loss in the five days, during which time we were exposed to the fire of the enemy, was 6 killed, 38 wounded and 10 missing. The conduct of the officers and men is worthy of all praise. The men who fought so bravely at Antietam and Fredericksburg forgot not their record, nor failed to add to it another page inscribed with glorious deeds of patriotic valor."

The move which he refers to, having been made in the dense wilderness—changing front to rear on 10th Company—was spoken of at the time as having been a masterly one on a small scale. A mind guided it that had retained its self-possession : he preserved his coolness during the heavy fire, and having caused his command to share his coolness, he extricated it from its position of peril and led it calmly from the field. These movements had been watched by superior officers and admired, and Major General French promptly recommended him for a Brigadier General, and used his efforts to secure the position for him.

During all of this series of movements, embracing several days, Colonel Smyth was prompt in the execution of all commands, failing not in the slightest detail, always observant, and withal full of fight : and by the time the operations had ceased, other commands than the 1st Delaware had remarked that Colonel Smyth had material

out of which soldiers are made, and that he was destined
to become an officer of mark.

Very shortly after this campaign, Colonel Smyth was
assigned to the command of the 2d Brigade, 3d Division,
2d army corps. Here a more extended field for the display of his military powers was offered him. Before,
he had but one Regiment to command : here he had five,
and it was correctly supposed that an officer who could
manipulate his own Regiment so skillfully and bring out
its prowess so strongly, would be very apt to succeed
with several organizations in a corresponding manner :
besides, there was another incentive : there was increased
responsibility, and this would necessitate increased labor
and watchfulness. He was equal to the duty, and never
appeared to question his own ability, feeling a certain
confidence in himself : and he was not mistaken in his
estimate of his powers, for there were few civilian Generals who could handle a Brigade with more skill or get
more fight out of it : on drill, on the march, or in an engagement, the freedom and ease with which he manœuvered it were apparent. Before he gave an order, he always knew precisely what he wanted to have accomplished, and he always saw that it was accomplished with the
utmost promptitude. With him, in military movement,
there was neither blunder nor delay, and when a commanding officer gave him an order, he knew it would be
executed if possible.

Gettysburg was the first engagement in which Smyth
had commanded a Brigade. Here he was conspicuous
for bravery, exposing himself at all points where he
thought his duty called him. Here General Alexander

Hays was in charge of the Division which held an important point, and Smyth was one of his Brigade commanders. On the third day of the fight, Pettigrew's Division which was opposed to Hays' Division, received in its advance upon the troops of the latter, what Swinton, in his History of the army of the Potomac has characterized as a *feu d' enfer*, and which fire caused the troops of the former to break in disorder leaving many prisoners behind. Smyth reports that in that conflict his Brigade captured nine stands of colors and many prisoners. There was no faltering among his men : he was ever present to inspire them and cheer : his intrepidity and zeal were communicated to his troops, and the enemy in his front suffered in consequence.

In the afternoon of the last day of the fight, he was wounded on the nose and head by fragments of shell ; the wound of the face bled profusely, and both wounds gave him no little pain; his face was considerably disfigured by the swelling, and he was weakened by the loss of blood ; but he remained on the field until Gen. Hays ordered him to leave for surgical assistance, telling him that any man who was bleeding as he was, was a fitter subject for the Hospital than for the field. Accordingly the Colonel sought his surgeon, and his wounds were soon dressed. It having been remarked to him that his profile was somewhat marred by the wound, the hero replied that he was perfectly willing to sacrifice his nose for the sake of his country, and that the injury was a slight matter as compared with the glorious victory just won.

Generals Hancock and Hays complimented him highly and recommended him for promotion at once: they ever after spoke in warmest terms of praise of Smyth, and had the greatest confidence in him.

Colonel Smyth did not ask for or desire a leave of absence on account of his wounds, but preferred to remain with the army, in view of the movements then in progress. The day following the fight he returned to the field, and in a few days resumed command of the Brigade, much to the delight of all of the troops, who had in the short time he had commanded them, become greatly attached to him.

During that summer he was taken quite ill with a remittent fever, at Bristorburg, Fauquier County, Va. and was sent home on a sick leave, but returned in time to take a very active part in the engagement at Bristow Station, and in the movements around Warrenton, Centreville and Culpepper.

At Mine Run there was no great amount of fighting. The labor of withdrawing the pickets during the night of the retreat was a very delicate and dangerous one : as the two armies were entrenched so near to each other it was essential to the success of the retrograde movement that there should be no blunder in the withdrawal of the pickets. Colonel Smyth volunteered to bring them off, and he did it successfully, and by hard marching overtook the main column before day light. This one act of his showed that he not only was not afraid of danger, but rather courted it.

At the close of this month, December, Colonel Smyth re-enlisted with the Regiment as a veteran, and the Command returned to Wilmington to enjoy a 30 days furlough. Whilst on this visit, he was the recipient of many marks of favor from his fellow citizens: he had modified his prospects sensibly since his departure from the state. His friends were becoming proud of the record he was making for himself, for he was the subject of frequent and complimentary newspaper paragraphs, and the correspondents of the Daily press were calling attention to his deeds in most flattering terms, and his fame had now become more than local.

On the night of January 25th, at a supper of the Burns' Anniversary, he was presented with a handsome sword, sash, belt and shoulder straps by some of his Wilmington friends and admirers: his Diary records the fact that the presentation speech was made by Mr. Roberts.

In the month of April 1864, the Potomac army which was encamped for the most part, about Stevensburgh, Va. was re-organized: Brigades having been very greatly reduced in strength, were merged into others, so that many Colonels who had been in command of Brigades were obliged to return to their Regiments. But the services of Colonel Smyth were too fully estimated to be thus dispensed with, and he was accordingly assigned to the Command of the Irish Brigade in the 1st Division, Gen. Barlow commanding. He retained this command until the 17th of May, when he was ordered to return to his former Division, the 2d, and take command of the 2d Brigade, General Carroll having been wounded. Whilst in command of the Irish Brigade, he fought it in the Wilderness and Spottsylvania.

A correspondent who was in that organization, when the charge was made on the enemy's works at Spottsylvania on the 12th of May, thus writes: "the Brigade, in solid column, marched up within three hundred yards of the jaws of death, and at a given signal, in one voice, gave vent to the round, full ringing Federal shout, and charged in the face of a storm of leaden hail. The movement was eminently successful, and reflects lasting credit upon the intrepid, the gallant Colonel Smyth, whose name is already written in letters of gold on the scroll of military fame. Standing at the head of the column where the charge was made, he was slightly wounded, and taken from the field. Thirty minutes had not elapsed when we were in the quiet possession of 22 pieces of cannon, 12 stands of colors and 8000 prisoners, including 2 Major Generals. The second Brigade may well feel proud of their officers. Colonel Smyth was born to command and be respected, and when he takes the lead, his valiant men follow his footsteps, no matter what impending barriers rise up to impede their progress. He is the man for the times, the man for the dangerous sphere where he is now engaged, not rash, but prudent, and firm as granite in time of danger, and for his strategic movements, he cannot be outflanked by older Generals in the field."

Though he had commanded the Irish Brigade but a few weeks, he had made his reputation with those troops before he left them. To show the sentiment which prevailed throughout that command with reference to him, we cannot do better than by quoting some of the pleasant testimonials he received. General Barlow thus expresses himself. "The General commanding the Division takes occasion to express his great regret at thus losing the services of Colonel Smyth. He desires to express in the strongest terms, his appreciation of the courage, skill and soldierly qualities of Colonel Smyth, his satisfaction at the success which that officer has had in improving the condition and discipline of his command in camp, and his gallantry in fighting it in the field. Colonel Smyth will be a valuable accession to any command."

The following lines were addressed to him by a member of the Irish Brigade upon his leaving that organization, and betrays the affection felt for him.

" Must friendship be strengthened by time ?
　Is the growth of affection so slow ?
Ah ! no 'tis a feeling sublime,
　Like the sun bursting forth in full glow.
Though few were the days you were here.
　Your memory never shall fade ;
No man on this earth is more dear.
　Than " Tom Smyth " of the Irish Brigade.

" Kind nature has marked on thy face.
　The virtues that glow in thy soul :
She gave thee courage and grace,
　The gallant to win and control ;
The Irishman's laugh from the heart,
　The tongue that no friend e'er betrayed :
Oh ! the boast and the model thou art.
　" Tom Smyth " of the Irish Brigade.

" Tom Smyth," proud Columbia can boast
　Of no soldier more loyal or true :
No star from her flag shall be lost.
　While she's guarded by heroes like you.
We grudge not our blood in her cause,
　Nor her young men beneath her turf laid :
But we'll fight for her union and laws,
　" Tom Smyth, " and the Irish Brigade.

" May come back sweet peace to this land ;
May love o'er her gallant sons reign !
May the North and the South hand in hand
Sweep all foes from the land and the main.
And then may we free our green home :
May her tyrants forever be laid !
And then may fair liberty bloom,
" Tom Smyth " and our Irish Brigade."

The following address was sent to Colonel Smyth
upon his departure from the Brigade, every officer of
which Brigade having signed the testimonial.

"IRISH BRIGADE, May 20, 1864.

COLONEL,

Your farewell address caused us mingled feelings
of regret and pride : regret, for it was the signal of the
departure of our loved and valued friend : pride, for it
told us our worth was estimated by one whose respect
we covet and whose sincerity we prize.

Long before your late connection with our Brigade,
we were in the habit of hearing your merits extolled as
a soldier and a gentleman, and the more we knew you,
the more we were convinced that the praise of your
many friends did not exceed your deserts.

You leave us after having led us on the battle field,
with a gallantry never before surpassed, and delighted us
in private by your frankness and cordiality. In you are
combined the loyal American, the patriotic Irishman and
the high-minded Gentleman. You are called away from
us, but our affections will follow you. You leave no fad-
ing memory in our hearts, and may the God of battles
preserve you for the glory of this great land, the freedom
of Ireland, and the happiness of your social circle. This

is the fervent prayer of every one in the Irish Brigade. Farewell."

With these men Colonel Smyth was the beau ideal of the Irish soldier and gentleman : dashing and brave, and with as kind a heart as ever throbbed ; in their estimation he embodied the gallantry of their race, and was the type of the manly, heroic and gentle. He could excite their enthusiasm and sway them as he willed, and it was always considered perfectly fitting that such a brave man should command such a brave Brigade of the same nationality.

It was at about this period that much indignation was felt among Smyth's military friends that he had not been promoted : they argued that he had already accomplished enough to entitle him to advancement: his merit had been fully recognized in the army, and recommendation after recommendation had been forwarded to the war Department, but he had no political influence that co operation might be secured, and it was a surprise with all that the politicians in Delaware who were perfectly conversant with the brilliant record he was making, did not interest themselves in his case. He had all the military influence requisite, for his standing in the army was a most advantageous one, and all that was wanting was some one to call the attention of the Department in a special manner to his claims. The Colonel was very sensitive and always felt this apparent neglect, but he was too modest ever to ask the good offices of any one in his favor. He felt that the politicians at home had ignored him entirely or had tried to do so, though it was impossible for them to remain in ignorance of his merits, for the papers and records were full of the deeds of the gallant Smyth: no fight occurred in which his name did not honorably appear, and it was impossible for any one who watched the journals, not to discover that there was one officer from Delaware who was making a large ripple in military circles, and who by his own unaided efforts was enforcing the recognition of his merits without much reason for gratitude to those whose pleasure it should have been to advance him.

The indignation of some of his friends at this neglectful treatment, found vent in poetry; Surgeon Reynolds of the Irish Brigade resolved itself in the following lines addressed to the Colonel.

" Though stars are falling very thick,
   On many a curious spot ;
And warrior rising very quick,
   Who never heard a shot.
Still though you periled limb and life,
   And many a fight went through,
And laurels won in every strife,
   There's not a star for you, Tom Smyth,
     There's not a star for you."

" 'Tis true, when close the hostile lines,
   The headlong charge you lead,
And your sword, glory's beacon, shines
   In front of your Brigade ;
But you can't like a courtier grin,
   No little work can do,
So you perchance a ball may win :
   But there's no star for you, Tom Smyth,
     But there's no star for you."

" Whene'er you tread the crimson sod,
   Your form and soul expand ;
In olden times you'd seem a god,
   Not Hancock's self more grand.

But than your sword, a wily tongue.
   Far greater deeds can do:
For while stars grace the gabby throng,
   There's not a star for you , Tom Smyth,
      There's not a star for you.''

" No coward in the ranks is seen
   When gallant Smyth appears,
Men kindle at his voice and mien,
   And move on with gay cheers.
Smyth's spirit moves the glowing mass,
   Deeds past their power they do ;
Yet while such things you bring to pass,
   There's not a star for you, Tom Smyth,
      There's not a star for you.''

" But by you for no selfish cause
   Is battle's flag unfurled,
You fight to save our glorious laws
   To bless the future world.
Brave Hancock owns you're skilled and brave,
   The army owns it too ;
Then the proud feeling you must have
   Is rank and star for you, Tom Smyth,
      Is rank and star for you.''

Having joined the 2d Division—Major General Gibbon commanding—whilst actively engaged in the movement that brought the army in front of Petersburg, there was no chance for him to be idle : all of his energies were called into play, and well did he acquit himself: he was in those continuous operations ceaseless in his efforts to keep his command up to the highest point of discipline and efficiency.

The following report is a history of his operations for more than two months.

     " HDQRS. 3D BRIGADE. 2D DIV. 2D ARMY CORPS.

        In the Field, August 29, 1864.

CAPT. A. H. EMBLER, A. A. A. G.

   CAPTAIN :—I have the honor to submit the following report of the operations of the Third Brigade from May 17. 1864, the date upon which I assumed command, to July 30, 1864, divided into four epochs, pursuant to special order No. 209, Headquarters army of the Potomac.

I.   I assumed command about 8.30 P. M. by order of Brigadier General Gibbon, the army then being in the vicinity of Spottsylvania Court House.   I was ordered to mass the Brigade in front of the Landrum House and near the vacated line of the enemy's entrenchments, before daylight; which was accomplished, the Brigade being in column of battalions between the house and the road.   Subsequently it was deployed into line by battalions in mass, and I was ordered by Brigadier General Gibbon to move forward in support of the Corcoran Legion.

At daylight the Legion moved forward, and I followed at a short supporting distance.   The first line was repulsed, and my Brigade, taking a position in a ravine, covered their retreat.   I at once deployed a line of skirmishers and held this position until 12.35 P. M., when in obedience to orders from General Gibbon, I withdrew to the second line of entrenchments where my command formed line of battle and rested.   At 10, P. M. the Brigade moved to Anderson's Mills where it took position.   On the morning of May 19th, the command went into camp, the 1st Delaware Volunteers being detailed for picket.   At 6 P. M. an order was received for the Brigade to march at once.   The Brigade moved quickly to the Fredericksburg road.   The order was soon countermanded, and the command returned to camp at Anderson's Mills.

II.   May 20th I received an order to move with my command at 11 P. M.   I moved at 11.20 P. M., taking the road toward Mattapony church, continuing the marching May 21st, passing Grimes' Station, passing through Milford and Bowling Green and crossing the Ny River where the command went into position, and threw up entrenchments, the 8th Ohio volunteers being detailed for picket.

May 22d, I received orders from General Gibbon to take my

Brigade and make a reconnoisance to develop the strength and position of the enemy. The Regiments composing the force were the 14th Connecticut, 7th Virginia, 14th Indiana, 10th New York, 12th New Jersey, 4th Ohio. The 1st Delaware and 10th New York were employed in erecting earth works. I deployed the 14th Indiana and 4th Ohio volunteers as skirmishers. One Lieutenant and twenty men of the 10th New York were placed on the right and rear of the skirmish line to protect that flank, and two companies of the 14th Connecticut were similarly placed to protect the left flank.

Colonel T. G. Ellis, 14th Connecticut volunteers and Lieut. Col. Carpenter, 4th Ohio volunteers, were assigned respectively to the command of the left and right wings of the skirmish line. Two companies of the 14th Connecticut were sent to reconnoitre the Hanover Junction Road.

The 12th New Jersey and 10th New York, were placed in support of artillery near the Cross Roads, and the 7th Virginia stationed near the Cross Roads. The skirmish line was then pushed forward about two miles, finding nothing but cavalry or mounted infantry to oppose them.

About 3 P. M. I received orders from Gen. Gibbon to halt, and I was subsequently ordered to assemble my command and return to camp. On May 23d, the command marched at 7 A. M. to the North Anna River where the enemy were discovered to be posted in force. At noon my Brigade was massed behind a ridge of hills. At 4 P. M., the 4th Ohio was deployed as skirmishers and moved to the river bank where it became engaged at once with the enemy on the opposite shore; it was relieved at dark by the 7th Virginia. At 7 P. M. I was ordered by Gen. Gibbon to make a demonstration against the Railroad Bridge across the river. I moved the 8th Ohio and 14th Indiana to the bridge, where they opened fire on the enemy's skirmishers during the night—my Brigade entrenched itself.

Shortly after midnight the enemy succeeded in burning the bridge. At 7 A. M. May 24, I received an order from Gen. Gibbon to construct a rough bridge and cross a Regiment as skirmishers. About 10.15 A. M. the bridge was completed and the 8th Ohio moved to the opposite side, deployed and advanced to the enemy's earthworks, which they occupied, the enemy having fallen back.

The remainder of the Brigade was then crossed and took position in line of battle.

At 3 P. M. I was ordered to advance and ascertain the position of the enemy. The 1st Delaware and 108th New York were deployed as skirmishers, and advanced about a half a mile, the left swinging forward. At this point the enemy offered a strong resistance, and I deployed the 14th Connecticut to strengthen the line.

I then moved forward again, but as the enemy were posted in rifle pits in the edge of a wood, while my skirmishers were obliged to pass on an elevated ploughed field, the line was again brought to a halt. I then addressed the 12th New Jersey to charge the enemy's rifle pits, which was done in fine style, the enemy being driven about five hundred yards. The enemy having been reinforced, I brought up the 7th Virginia and 10th New York to strengthen the left centre of my line. The pressure still continuing strongest at this point, and the 19th Maine having reported to me, I ordered it also to that part of the line.

Learning that the enemy were moving troops towards my right. I directed the 8th and 4th Ohio and 14th Indiana to take position to cover the right flank of my line of battle. At 5.30 P. M. the enemy made a determined attack on my centre. The 69th and 170th New York, which had reported to me, were brought in to strengthen this part of the line, and the 4th and 8th Ohio and 14th Indiana were moved from the right to the centre. This attack of the enemy was handsomely repulsed. The 15th and 19th Massachusetts having reported to me, I directed them to form on the right, relieving the 12th New Jersey, 1st Delaware, 108th New York and 7th Virginia, which Regiments were formed in the rear and re-supplied with ammunition. The 69th Pennsylvania reporting to me at this time, was formed on the left of my line of battle.

Just at dark a vigorous attack was made by the enemy on my left, which threw the 67th and 170th New York into considerable disorder, which resulted in their falling back. I succeeded in rallying them, however, and formed that part of the line at right angles with the main line. During the night my command threw up entrenchments. On the morning of the 25th, the first line was pushed forward with but little opposition, and on the right, breastworks were erected in advance of the previous position. The first line now consisted, from right to left, of the 7th Virginia, 108th New York, 1st Delaware, 8th Ohio, 12th New Jersey, 14th Connecticut, 69th Pennsylvania, and 170th N. Y. The 4th Ohio, 14th Indiana and 10th New York were in the second line. At dark the 4th Ohio and 14th Indiana were moved by me to Doswell House, to cover the left flank of my position.

At 5 P. M. May 26th I received orders from Gen. Gibbon to advance my skirmish line by swinging forward the left, and to dislodge a force of the enemy who held a salient position near the left of my line. At dark, I pushed forward the 69th Pennsylvania, 170th New York, and two companies of the 14th Connecticut, who charged the enemy and drove him from his position. Soon after I received an order from Gen. Gibbon to be prepared to recross the North Anna. At 8 P. M., the Brigade moved across the river and bivouacked until morning.

III. On May 27, the command marched to within a mile of Haunquartus Creek, where it bivouacked for the night. At noon May 28, we crossed the Pamunky River. At 1 P. M., I received an order to fall on the cavalry, which was subsequently countermanded, and my Brigade filed into the field on the left of the road and took position in two lines of battle. On May 29th, I was directed to swing forward the left of my command, now about a half a mile to the front, form line of battle and entrench. Subsequently I was ordered to hold the command in readiness to march at short notice. At 5.30 A. M., May 30th, the command marched acting as reserve. At 9.25 A. M., I was ordered to move further to the front. My Brigade was then formed in line of battle near the Jones' House. The 7th Virginia was directed to drive the enemy's Sharpshooters from a house about five hundred yards in front of my left flank, which they quickly accomplished. On May 31st, I received orders to be in readiness to support the 1st Brigade. At 1 P. M. the command was marched across Tolopotomy Creek and massed in rear of the 1st Brigade. At 2 P. M. the 108th New York and 7th Virginia were sent to the support of the right.

At dark, the 14th Connecticut, 8th Ohio, and 12th New Jersey were formed in an interval between the 1st and 2d Brigades. Soon after dark, the 8th Ohio was relieved, and returned to its original position. At 12.25 P. M., June 1st, I was ordered by Gen. Gibbon to be in readiness to march at once. This order was subsequently countermanded, and the Brigade threw up entrenchments. At dark, I was directed to occupy the earthworks, and relieve the First Brigade. At 9 P. M., the Brigade marched taking the road to Coal Harbor, which place it reached June 2d. At 2.20 P. M., June 2d, my Brigade was deployed in line of battle and by order of Gen. Gibbon advanced to a vacated line of rifle pits, where it took position under a severe fire from the enemy's skirmishers, who were concealed in rifle pits within short range of my right. At 5 P. M., I was ordered to attack the enemy's position, but the attack was subsequently deferred. The 184th Pennsylvania reported to me, and was placed on the extreme right of my line.

During the night sharp skirmishing occurred on my right. At 4.30 A. M., June 3d, I was ordered to attack the enemy. I formed my Brigade in line of battle and advanced and charged the enemy's works. When the command arrived at from sixty to one hundred yards from the enemy's works, the ranks had become so thinned and the fire from the enemy's artillery and musketry was so destructive that the men were compelled to halt, and seek such shelter as presented itself. In this position, the command soon erected a rude breastwork. At 9 A. M., Berdan's Sharpshooters and a battalion of the First Massachusetts Heavy Artillery reported to me. I deployed part of the Sharpshooters in front of skirmishers and held the battalion of First Massachusetts Heavy Artillery in reserve. At 4 P. M., the 164th New York, and the remaining battalion of 1st Massachusetts reported to me, which Regiments I formed on the opposite side of the ravine on my extreme right. My line strengthened their works, and was arranged from right to left, as follows :—1st Massachusetts, 164th New York, 14th Connecticut, 8th Ohio, 4th Ohio, 7th Virginia, 12th New Jersey, 10th New York, 1st Delaware, 14th Indiana.

About 8 P. M., the enemy opened upon us a terrible artillery fire, which lasted about thirty minutes, after which he charged along my whole line. He was repulsed with considerable loss. During the night one-half the command were kept awake and under arms. In this action Lieutenant Benjamin Y. Draper, A. A. D. C., on my staff, a brave and gallant young officer, was killed At 10.30 A. M., June 4th, the enemy opened on us a heavy artillery fire, which continued until 11.35, doing but little injury. Sharp skirmishing was kept up all day. At 8.40 P. M., the brisk skirmish changed to a very heavy musketry fire on both sides, followed by a short artillery duel, which did no damage to my Brigade, except the wounding of one of my staff orderlies, private James Kay, 10th New York. Severe skirmishing continued all day.

June 5th, in the afternoon, my standard bearer, Private Elliott, 10th New York, was mortally wounded whilst carrying an order. At 8.30 P. M., the enemy commenced a vigorous attack with artillery and musketry, which lasted twenty-four minutes without doing injury. Heavy skirmishing continued during June 6th and until 4 P. M. June 7th, when a cessation of hostilities was ordered, to give opportunity to bury the dead. During the 8th and 9th of June, there was very little skirmishing. and on the 10th my command was relieved from duty in the entrenchments. There was skirmishing all day June 11th. At dark June 12th, the command marched to the left.

IV. The Brigade marched all day, June 13th, and encamped near Wilcox's Landing on James River. About dark, June 14th, we crossed James River on transports and encamped at Windmill Point. At 10.30 A. M., June 15th, the Brigade moved towards Petersburg, and about 10 P. M., relieved the troops of the 18th Army Corps. Skirmishing during the 16th.

On June 17th, I was ordered to report with my command to Gen. Barlow. On June 18th, I took position at daylight, and at 4 A. M., advanced upon the enemy's position and discovered that he had fallen back about half a mile. During the day the Brigade charged twice. After skirmishing during the 19th and 20th, the command was relieved and marched to the left, about three miles and encamped. At 8 A. M., June 21st, the Brigade marched and took position on the left of Jerusalem Plank road, where the enemy was found entrenched. In this position we threw up breastworks.

At 3 P. M., June 22d, the enemy attacked the troops on our left, turned the flank of the first line and captured a battery and many prisoners. On the 23d, the enemy vacated the line of works they had captured. On June 24th, my command moved to the rear, and relieved some of the 5th Corps. We remained in this position until June 27th. when the Brigade was deployed to picket the rear of the army, remaining on picket until June 29th, when I was ordered to move to the entrenchments of the 6th Corps.

On July 2d, the command moved to the right, and on the 11th commenced tearing down the breast-works in front of them. On July 12th, my Brigade was on picket, and continued on that duty until the morning of July 15th, when they were relieved by troops of the 5th Corps, and went into the rear of the Southall House. In the evening of the 15th, the command marched to Haines' House and commenced to tear down the old rebel works in the vicinity, returning to camp on the morning of the 16th. The Brigade remained in Camp until July 21st, when they were set to work making a covered way in the rear of the 5th Corps entrenchments.

On July 22d, the Brigade moved into the entrenchments previously occupied by Ferrero's Division of Colored troops, remaining in these works until July 26th, when at 3.30 P. M., the command was massed near Corps Headquarters, and at 4.25 moved off towards the Appomatox, which river we crossed on pontoons during the night. At daylight on the 27th, the Brigade crossed the James River, and were soon engaged in skirmishing with the enemy. On July 28th, my command marched to support the cavalry, and at dark took up a new position and entrenched. During the night of the 29th, we marched back to the vicinity of Petersburg, and at daylight were massed in the rear of the 5th Corps. After the explosion of the mine and the failure of the assault on the enemy's works, the command returned to camp near the Southall House.

The loss of the Brigade during the campaign, including the battle of the Wilderness, when Col. Carroll was in command, is as follows :—

COMMISSIONED OFFICERS—Killed,		·	·		22
	Wounded,	·	·	·	12
	Missing,	·	·	·	9
ENLISTED MEN—Killed,	·	·		·	254
	Wounded.		·		1320
	Missing,	·		·	289

Total number of casualties:

Commissioned officers,	· · · ·	103
Enlisted men,	· · · ·	1852
Grand total.	· · · ·	1955

The conduct of both officers and men during the campaign, has been in every respect unexceptionable. It is a source of extreme gratification to me to be able to recommend to the Major General commanding the Division, the gentlemen of my staff, for the prompt and efficient manner in which they executed all my orders. Their gallantry on the field of battle has seldom been surpassed.

Very Respectfully,

Your obedient servant.

THOMAS A. SMYTH.

Colonel Commanding Third Brigade, 2d Division, 2d Army Corps.

On July 9th, Col. Smyth was placed temporarily in command of the Division. This was a mark of confidence, since there was a Colonel in the same Division who ranked him. Whilst in command, he invited on a certain Sabbath the various ministers of the Division to come to his headquarters, and sent orders to the Brigade Commanders to bring their commands over, that religious services might be held. He wished that his example might be good, and if possible the religious sense of the soldiers stimulated. Immense coverings of pine boughs screened the assemblage from the sun, and the pine browse on the ground afforded soft and lowly seats. All the Bands in the Division were present and gave fine music, and the officers led in the singing. The prayers were fervent and appropriate, and the remarks from the different ministers were well adapted to the circumstances of time and place, and there were few in that congregation who did not feel the happy influences of those Sabbath services.

The following is taken from his Diary, as the record of some facts concerning the second Deep Bottom fight.

"August 14, at 9 A. M. the Division was disembarked and massed in the rear of the works erected by us on the 30th of July. At 11 o'clock I received orders to march to the front, posting one Brigade on the New Market Road, the 2d on the—road: the first Brigade I massed on the right, and at 4 oclock I charged the enemy's works, but owing to a deep ditch and a tangled mass of briers, it was found impossible to get through: at dark I had the Brigade withdrawn, and massed the Division in rear of 2d Brigade." "On the 15th at 3.30 o'clock I withdrew the command a short distance to the rear, leaving a strong picket line in front. At dark I relieved the 1st Division picket and placed Colonel Murphey's Brigade in the breastwork. The 10th Corps was to attack at 5 o'clock, but from some unaccountable reason, the attack did not take place." "August 16th. They are to attack some time to-day. I sent the 3d Brigade to report to Gen. Birney. When Birney made the attack, I made a demonstration from the left and right of my line. the 7th Michigan on the left and the 2d Brigade on the right with a section of Dow's Battery in the centre. I drew the enemy to my front."

It will have been observed that during all these operations, Smyth was commanding the Division, Major Gen. Gibbon being absent, and the impression was general, that if an important engagement should come off, the Colonel would do his utmost to demonstrate his ability to handle a Division, and no one questioned the result of the effort.

The Battle of Reams Station followed quickly on the heels of these movements, and we cannot do better than let him tell the part he took in it.

"August 24th, at 3 A. M. took up our line of march for Reams Station and formed line on the left of the 1st Division. At 7½ o'clock, I occupied the works of the 1st Division, and posted my pickets. At dark I closed to the right to give way to that Division; orders to march at 5.30 A. M. to guard the working party." "August 25, I received orders to march out the Rail Road: the enemy appeared in force in our front on the road. I received orders to deploy one of my Regiments as skirmishers—1st Delaware—and support it by the 12th New Jersey. I moved forward about half a mile, driving in the enemy's cavalry videttes. My right flankers reported the enemy on m7 right. I had the 10th New York deployed to protect my flank. I advanced about a mile driving the enemy to their works, but found it impossible to cross the swamp in their front I fell back a short distance, taking position behind a rail fence when the enemy charged me, but was handsomely repulsed by my line of skirmishers. I soon after received an order from Gen. Gibbon to make another attack and find out what was in my front. I deployed the 7th Virginia and 14th Connecticut, supported on the left flank by the 12th New Jersey, 69th Pennsylvania in the rear and 10th New York on the right. I charged again to the swamp, and found it impossible to cross under the heavy fire. I fell back to the fence where I remained until I received orders from Major Gen. Gibbon to bring my command back to the works. By this time I was very nearly surrounded but succeeded in finding a gap and brought the Brigade in safely. I was posted by Major Gen. Gibbon on the left of the 2d Brigade, where I erected a work. The enemy made three charges on the 1st Division and were repulsed.

They then opened a most destructive fire of artillery which

took my line right in the rear, followed by a charge on the 1st Division, and struck a Regiment of " Heavy's " who broke, giving up the work to the rebels. I faced my Brigade about and charged through the corn field and up the hill to the other side, but the men being so much exhausted from the operations of the morning they fell out on the way : by the time I got to the hill, I had so few left that I was repulsed. I fell back to my old works. The enemy having captured 12 pieces of artillery, the 12d New Jersey, 14th Connecticut and 10th New York recaptured three of them : about 6½ o'clock they attacked the 2d Brigade on my right : they fell back along my rear carrying the greater portion of my men along with them : the balance of my command I formed in the edge of the wood in the rear of the 1st Division : I took the 69th Pennsylvania to the front to bring off the 3 guns, but on the way I found they were being brought off by some of the men on the left of the 1st Division. I posted the 69th Pennsylvania to protect the left flank of the three Regiments I had on the 1st Division left. "

In September he was again in command of the Division about three weeks, Major General Gibbon having been temporarily assigned to the command of the 18th army corps.

On October 1st 1864, Thomas A. Smyth was commissioned Brigadier General. The evening that his commission was received by him was one to be remembered. The Division was in the trenches in front of Petersburg, and the gratifying intelligence was speedily conveyed to it. All were enthusiastic over the event. Staff officers and others called upon him immediately, and congratulations poured in upon him from all quarters. The Division staff wishing to testify their satisfaction at his well earned promotion, sent a man at once to City Point, directing him to purchase the finest pair of

shoulder straps that could be found in that mart. Within three hours the man returned with the present, and
found the General at Division Headquarters, beaming
with pleasure at his advancement and the general joy
manifested. The shoulder straps were at once presented
much to his astonishment. (So deeply was he moved by
this slight testimonial that at first he was unable to utter
a word : a tear gathered in his eye, and at last he feeling-
ly remarked "Gentlemen, I had no right to expect this.")

Early in the night the welcome news reached the
troops in the trenches, forts, and on the picket lines, and
such a shout as was set up by those enthusiastic admirers of this brave man, was seldom ever heard along those
lines : the cheering lasted nearly an hour, extending the
entire Division line, and being taken up by the pickets.
So hearty were the cheers and so prolonged, that the
enemy inquired as to the occasion of them. Throughout
the camps of the Brigade it was a season of jollification,
and upon the whole, the manner in which the news of
the promotion was received there, was flattering in the
extreme.

Measures were at once taken by the troops to show
in a more material shape their appreciation of the honor
conferred upon their popular commander.

The following address was delivered to the General
on the 17th of October by the non-commissioned officers
and privates of the 63d Regiment, New York State Volunteers, Irish Brigade.

"GENERAL,
              We come this day to express our delight at your
well-earned promotion and to bear with us our offering of affection.

We have purchased for you a powerful war-horse, and with our warmest wishes for your welfare and prosperity, we give him to his new master.

Ours is indeed the widow's gift—the non-commissioned officers and privates of the 63d Regiment—Irish Brigade; we have not rank or wealth, and you knowing it, will prize our offering as much as the most costly.

We have no connection with you, as our Brigade is not now under your command, but the ties of affection still remain and will forever. We found in you a strict disciplinarian, but you had the singular felicity of combining mildness of manner with firmness of purpose, and we endured with pleasure every labor you commanded, for we knew your lofty motives and your love for us.

Brave, courteous and humane, you bring before our eyes, a living portrait of the Irish hero of yore, and may the day come, when after preserving the glorious union of this land, you will lead us across the ocean to raise to independence and happiness our own dear, unforgotten Ireland."

On the 22d he was the recipient of a still more handsome present. The Brigade without his knowledge had sent an agent to Washington who purchased a saddle, bridle, saddle cloth, breast strap, saddle bags, holsters, sword, sash, belt and shoulder straps, all of the most exquisite workmanship, and costing nearly twelve hundred dollars; and the First Delaware had purchased for him a splendid horse.

On the morning of the day on which the presentation was to be made, he was influenced to leave his Head quarters for a few hours in order that time might be given to arrange the surprise for him. During his absence the presents were all arranged in a tent, and the horse was dressed in the handsome trappings. When the General returned from his ride, he was astonished to see nearly every officer of the Brigade and many of the enlisted men in front of his tent: he inquired very innocently and naturally what the occasion for the assemblage was, when he was conducted to the tent where the presents were displayed; the horse was led out gaily caparisoned, and the General was persuaded to mount in order to test the qualities of the animal. The General in a pleasant vein acknowledged the gifts, and some witty speeches followed in which he was duly lauded: the greatest enthusiasm prevailed, and every man present felt proud of the General, and that he deserved every favor and compliment he had received. Nothing was ever done grudgingly for him.

The following account of the engagement at Hatcher's Run October 27th, is taken from his Diary.

"Orders to march at 3 A. M.: my Brigade in advance: rode with a squad of cavalry leading: surprised and drove the rebel videttes in: at Cedar creek we were checked by a strong force of rebs: my Brigade formed in line of battle and charged, wading the creek to their arm pits and carried the works in fine style, pushing the enemy and advancing in good order. After crossing the open field, we halted the command and formed the line again, putting the 1st Delaware out as skirmishers, who advanced and drove the enemy three fourths of a mile. We then took the road to Anderson's Mills, the 1st Brigade in advance: were put in position by Major Gen. Hancock, and deployed the 4th Company of the 14th Connecticut as skirmishers and charged a Battery which limbered up and left. I soon after received orders to support the 2d Brigade, and advance to the mill on the right of the road. Orders to form on right of

2d Brigade, and while performing this movement, the rebels advanced and drove the cavalry back. I ordered the 1st Delaware by the left flank and charged the rebel line, following them to the Creek and taking their works: this position I held all day, subject to a fire from all flanks."

His modesty influenced him, in this account to omit mention of his own deeds, but his old command will not forget the gallant style in which he dashed into the creek, waving his hat in his hand, and cheering the men on by his example; the enemy fled in confusion, and he at the head of his troops spurred on after them. Major Gen. Hancock, in a letter written long after, spoke of Smyth as having on this occasion, "led his command in the most dashing manner."

A few days after the conclusion of this movement, the General having applied for a short leave of absence, received it; his object was to join the masonic order, which he did whilst in Wilmington.

In the latter part of November he was again assigned to the temporary command of the Division, and again in December. As Gen. Gibbon was shortly after assigned to the command of the 24th Army Corps, it was now hoped by all that Smyth would retain command of the Division, but on the 25th of February, Gen. William Hayes a senior Brigadier was assigned, and Smyth returned to the command of the Brigade, but not until he had manœuvered the Division in the series of movements about Hatcher's Run, embracing the 5th, 6th and 7th of February.

His report says:

" On the 5th at 7 A. M. we took up our line of march, 1st

2d and 3d Brigades. 300 cavalry reported to me and the 10th New York Battery. We took the road to Armstrong's Mills, driving the enemy's videttes and skirmishers across Hatcher's Run. I took up position with my left resting on the run, and right on the swamp, with the 20th Massachusetts and 69th Pennsylvania volunteers on the right. The enemy opened several times through the day with artillery, but we did not reply to them. In the afternoon at 4.30, they made a fierce attack on the 20th Massachusetts and 69th Pennsylvania, driving them in; the 3d Brigade of the 3d Division formed in their rear with the 12th New Jersey; the attack was gallantly repulsed."

" February 6th at 4 P. M. the 5th Corps made a reconnoisance to Burgess' Mill, and after a sharp fire of musketry they fell back to their old position, followed closely by the enemy. when my left became engaged: Smyth's Battery did good execution."

Major General Humphreys commanding the 2d Corps at that time, in a printed general order says, in speaking of the operations, " while all did their duty. some were favored by fortune in being placed at the points against which the enemy's efforts were concentrated, and were thus afforded the opportunity of displaying conspicuously their soldierly qualities. Among those favored were Brigadier General Smyth, commanding 2d Division, Brevet Brigadier General McAllister commanding 3d Brigade, 3d Division, and Col. Matthew Murphy, commanding 2d Brigade, 2d Division.

The enemy concentrated a powerful force, composed of parts of two corps—Hill's and Gordon's on the right of Smyth—Murphy's Brigade and the artillery—and in front of McAllister, and made a determined effort to break our line. They were skillfully and gallantly met

and repulsed with severe loss to them and slight to us."
It was during this winter when encamped along
Hatcher's Run that he made himself a conspicuous target
for the enemy's pickets. One afternoon whilst riding
along outside of our picket line with a staff officer, making an informal reconnoisance on his own responsibility,
he was fired upon at very close range by two or three of
the enemy's pickets, and barely escaped the shots : the
night following, some of these same men deserted to our
lines and were brought to Division Headquarters. Whilst
their names were being taken, one of the men having
scanned the General very critically, exclaimed, " why
you are the very General I shot at this afternoon." He
added that the mark was so good, and the temptation of
putting out of the way a handsome Union General Officer
was too great to resist. The General had been shot at
so frequently in his rides along the picket line, and in the
skirmishes where he so often led, that he began to have
some faith in his invulnerability.

Now commenced the last of the many campaigns in
which he had participated. In his Diary for March 25th,
he says :

" 6 A. M. orders to be in readiness to march at a moments'
notice. 2 P. M., I took 500 men of my own Brigade and made an
attack on the rebel right, charged through the creek, carried their
works and took some prisoners." " March 29th at 6 A. M., I left
camp in advance of the Division ; the 7th Michigan reported to me ;
I marched out the Vaughn Road and took up position to the right
of that road." March 30th advanced at 6 A. M.: my Brigade in
reserve : the enemy fell back behind their line of works over Hatcher's Run : we took up position over the creek, right resting on the

" run," connecting with the 2d Division, 24th Corps: raining in torrents all day and night."

" March 31st at 1 A. M. I moved my Brigade to the left and behind McAllister's. Very heavy firing on the left; orders to advance all along the line at 11 A. M. I advanced my line and drove the enemy behind their works: slashing heavy along their works: impossible to get through at dark back to the line.

"April 1st, at 5 o'clock my Brigade was placed in reserve: at 7 o'clock I received orders to report to Gen. Mott and commenced the movement when I received orders to return to my old position."

"April 2d, I received orders to assault the enemy's works at 4 o'clock A. M. 3 o'clock orders countermanded: orders to report to Gen. Mott; heavy artillery and musketry along the line all night. The enemy left the works at 10 o'clock: marched to near Petersburg: at 2 o'clock took the " Fox Hill" road to Sheridan and the 5th Corps: bivouacked on the South Side Road. " April 3d orders to return towards Petersburg at sunrise: remained until 11½ and then took the road towards Lynchburg: at 10 P. M. bivouacked." " April 4th orders to march at 6 A. M.; took up our line of march at 7. April 5th at 8 o'clock took up the march for the Danville Rail Road, and took up position at the left of the 5th Corps at Jetersville Station. April 6th, orders to march at 5 A. M., and at 6 o'clock to assault the enemy's works."

This was the last line he ever wrote in his Diary. During that day there were continuous movements of troops, and on the following morning—the 7th, the skirmish began at " High Bridge."

The passage of the stream spanned by this Rail Road Bridge was disputed by the enemy, and there was some little difficulty experienced in their dislodgement; but after a short time, a passage was effected, though the immense structure and a smaller bridge for carriages, had been fired: the fire on the latter was extinguished before any damage was done, but several spans of the former were destroyed. A large number of guns were captured across the stream, and the enemy was promptly pursued; the Brigade of Smyth in advance, constantly engaging the enemy till Farmville was reached.

A short distance from that Town our forces had been temporarily checked by the heavy fire from the rebel artillery and sharpshooters. The General was in advance with the skirmish line as was his frequent custom, as he always wished to form an intelligent conception as to what was transpiring. He was mounted, with his staff about him: it was now about 11 o'clock in the morning, with a cold, disagreeable rain falling. There was an irregular fire of musketry going on. Suddenly he was seen to fall on the right side of his horse; his staff quickly dismounted and caught him: he was laid down, and it was discovered that he had been hit by a rebel sharpshooter. A small conical ball had entered the left side of the face, about an inch from the mouth, cutting away a tooth: the ball continued its course to the neck, fracturing a cervical vertebra, and driving a fragment of the bone upon the spinal cord: entire paralysis resulted. He was at once placed upon a stretcher and tenderly moved by a relay of sorrowing men to a farm house in the vicinity where the Corps Hospital was established, and where he received all the attention possible.

On the following morning—the 8th—he was started in a very comfortable ambulance to Burkesville Station—

distant about 12 miles, as it was not deemed wise to keep him in that region when the army was in rapid motion. A Surgeon and his two aids—Lieutenants Nones and Tanner were sent with him, and he was rendered as comfortable as circumstances permitted. He commenced failing sensibly by the time he had reached the residence of Col. Burke—about two miles from the station. The General, conscious that he was rapidly sinking, requested the party to stop with him there, saying that it was all over with him, and there was no use in his going any further. Col. Burke and family showed the General the greatest kindness and care, and this gentle soldier, never forgetting what was due to those about him, was so considerate and gentlemanly in his last hours, as to thank Col. Burke and family, just a short time before his death, for their hospitality and kindness to him and his attendants, telling them that he hoped that they would be rewarded.

At 4 o'clock on the morning of the 9th, he died as he had lived—a hero : he was perfectly resigned to his fate. Conscious within a very short period before his decease, he talked calmly. Not a groan or complaint had escaped him. He showed no emotion, but as a stoic endured the reflection that his once powerful, vigorous frame was but a complete wreck of humanity liable at any moment to be engulfed. When in an interview with his Surgeon as to the prospects of his case, he was informed as to the chances against his recovery, he remarked that if one man in a hundred recovered under a like injury, he should be that man—thus showing his determination. He added " now, Doctor, you know I am no coward, and that I am not afraid to die," and throughout he spoke calmly about passing away.

His body was removed the same day to Burkesville and embalmed, and at the expiration of two days was transmitted to Wilmington for interment.

He was the last General officer on the Union side killed in the war, was the last man wounded in the old Division which he had so ably commanded, and he died on the day of Lee's surrender. He had had three staff officers killed, and three horses shot under him.

To say that a deep gloom overspread not only his old command, but all others that knew him, would be but a feeble tribute to his worth. When it was known that Smyth was mortally wounded, and would never again appear on the field, strong men wept: men who were not accustomed on any occasion to evince much feeling, wept for the untimely fate of the brave man who had led them on so many bloody fields: in the operations which were now culminating in the overthrow of treason, they would miss his inspiring presence, his commanding form, his dashing style and his hearty salutation. The hero whom they had loved with such a manly love, and whom they would have followed wherever he led, was stricken and was surely dying, and sincere and profound was their grief. With these men he would never need anything to perpetuate his memory: his daring bravery and deeds of gallantry would embalm him there.

The sad event served to mar the general joy derived from the series of victories which our army was gaining, and in the midst of the rejoicings, the thought would obtrude itself "how mournful that Smyth was not there to receive the inspiration of events!" But he had fought his last fight, and bequeathed to his old command the remembrance of his gallant acts.

All the General and other officers who knew him or knew of him, expressed in the most feeling manner, their sense of the loss the army had sustained, and those with whom he had served were the most sensible of this loss.

The question has been asked by those who did not enjoy an acquaintance with General Smyth, and who were surprised to see him emerge so abruptly from a condition of obscurity, as it were, and take an enviable position before the military world with an ease and grace that appeared native to him—in what did his power consist, and by what means did he secure such a decided hold upon the minds and hearts of the people that he came in contact with?

It would be difficult to analyze with precision this force, and it would be safer to say that his influence was attained by means of a combination of elements that blended with no little harmony. Circumstances did much to develop in him the character of a hero, but much of the development process was due to himself and the judicious employment of the agencies that were available: to aid him, he had unusual force of character: a strong, vigorous mind that quickly received the impress of things that would be of practical utility in his line of duty, true nobility of soul that impressed all who came in his way, and a remarkable energy that convinced all that he was in earnest.

The great lever that served to elevate him was his

acknowledged gallantry. Many well fought fields attested his intrepid character. His was no brute courage: if he had a contempt for danger, it was not because he did not appreciate it, but because he felt he was able to meet it in any shape, and be proof against any demoralization: he reviewed the possible consequences in the spirit of a philosopher, and his noble devotion to the cause inspired him with the valor to face them as he did his foes. His place in the fray was always in the front, and he took a peculiar pride in thus posting himself and watching with absorbing interest the ever shifting scenes of a field of battle, and his troops seeing him there felt an increasing confidence and a desire to appear to advantage to his watchful eye. No fear under these circumstances when shot and shell were hurtling about, ever marked his bearing: not an emotion was betrayed on his countenance: he was calm and placid, always retaining his self possession, giving and executing orders with the same coolness that he showed on a dress parade.

He was never known to shirk a duty or danger, but always entered upon one or the other with the greatest alacrity, as though he were fond of them. He was conscientious in the discharge of every labor assigned him, and no slight obstacle was allowed to interfere with its execution, and his own comfort he never considered, and under any inflictions very rarely did he lose his amiability.

While his gallantry peculiarly fitted him for a soldier, with a natural aptitude for the business of a military life, he had a certain stoicism which together with his great physical endurance enabled him to offer a good example in bearing uncomplainingly, fatigue, exposure and privations. His physique was splendid, and indicated vigorous health and fine muscular development, and there was the utmost symmetry of form: every action denoted the highest state of vitality. He was military in his bearing, and looked the perfect soldier.

Though not a martinet, he possessed much system in his military government, and always succeeded in disciplining troops without undue harshness, and bringing out their fighting qualities very prominently. He had the faculty of order and could bring up a command to a desirable point of efficiency very readily. Witness his power over the Irish Brigade which became perfectly plastic in his hands.

So marked was the change that was effected in that command by his rule in a very brief period after he was assigned to it, that he was complimented in a very handsome manner by the Division commander. Again, the First Delaware owed much of the morale which distinguished it in its entire service to his leadership: he imparted to it zeal and confidence, and assisted it to make its reputation by inspiring it with his own gallantry. He delighted in the fame of the old Regiment even after he left it, and took the warmest interest in all that concerned it.

Much of his strength was in the fact that he was a gentleman in every sense of the word. His sense of delicacy was so nice, his native refinement so acute that he was seldom or never heard to utter a sentence that was calculated to offend the most fastidious: he was scrupulously correct in the style of his language: in all companies met together for sociality in the field where mirth reigned, he was, though genial as any, always dignified to a certain extent, and always the gentleman. His characteristic propriety of expression was not studied: it was natural indeed, and was but the reflex of a mind capable of originating nothing that was gross or of a debasing tendency. An inborn politeness and conscientious regard for the feelings of others, guided him in all of his relations with his fellow-men.

Though of no high educational culture, there were few men who could appear to greater advantage in society of gentlemen. Courteous in his manner, genial in his style, his habits of close observation, his acute perceptions, his naturally strong and vigorous mind, his readiness to talk, his faculty of readily comprehending, with his travels and varied experiences, made amends in a great measure for the deficiencies in his early education. In almost any society he would have been accepted, without question, as a cultured gentleman.

There was a certain magnetism of manner about him to which all yielded: it was a force of fascination which he had in a pre-eminent degree, and which was remarkable in one who had enjoyed no greater advantages of early life than he had. All who came within the sphere of this influence, felt and acknowledged this quality. It was a moral force that made for him friendships and attachments that sometimes partook of the

G

romantic. As the embodiment of all that was noble and generous in human nature, one could not help being attracted. Any one could see in him true nobility of soul, heroism of the most exalted kind, and a chivalry that adorned.

Add to these qualities, a modesty as great as his valor, and a life of unselfishness, swayed by the purest of motives, and it may be asked, is it surprising that he was a popular officer and man, and that he had such hosts of friends who took a warm personal interest in his welfare, and that such an eminence in the military world should have been accorded him ?

Such to his revered memory is the tribute conveyed in this simple narrative, from one friend whose long and intimate army acquaintance with the deceased, was the basis for an admiration and love enduring.